THE SPIDERWICK CHRONICLES

THIMBLETACK'S MISSION

by Rebecca Frazer
based on the screenplay by
Karey Kirkpatrick and David Berenbaum and John Sayles
from the books by
Tony DiTerlizzi and Holly Black

Ready-to-Read

Simon Spotlight
New York   London   Toronto   Sydney

SIMON SPOTLIGHT
An imprint of Simon & Schuster Children's Publishing Division
1230 Avenue of the Americas, New York, New York 10020
TM & © 2008 Paramount Pictures. All rights reserved.
All rights reserved, including the right of
reproduction in whole or in part in any form.
SIMON SPOTLIGHT, READY-TO-READ, and colophon are registered
trademarks of Simon & Schuster, Inc.
Manufactured in the United States of America
First Edition
10 9 8 7 6 5 4 3 2 1
CIP data for this book is available from the Library of Congress.
ISBN 13: 978-1-4169-4949-7
ISBN 10: 1-4169-4949-6

A long time ago, Arthur Spiderwick kept a record of his findings about a world of unseen creatures. He called this book *Arthur Spiderwick's Field Guide to the Fantastical World Around You.* What he wrote about was so powerful that the book had to be protected.

So Arthur asked his most trusted friend, a brownie named Thimbletack, to be the guardian of the Guide.

A very smart man, Arthur knew that if the Guide fell into the wrong hands, there would be trouble.

"We must protect the book!" he warned.

And Thimbletack made it his mission to do just that—no matter what! As long as he was around, the Guide would never leave Spiderwick Mansion.

Thimbletack took this important task very seriously. In fact, if you look up the meaning of "fiercely loyal" in the Field Guide, you will find a picture of Thimbletack! Of course, like all common house brownies, Thimbletack could turn into a boggart when he got angry, but Arthur knew that Thimbletack was anything but *common*!

For a long time Thimbletack's job was easy. Arthur, and later his daughter, Lucinda, went away, and the mansion was just how he liked it—clean and quiet!

It stayed that way until one dreadful night. It was the night the Grace family moved in—and Thimbletack's world was suddenly turned upside down!

Thimbletack saw that there were four Graces: the mother, Helen; a girl named Mallory; and twin boys, Jared and Simon. From the minute they arrived, they were loud *and* messy!

When Thimbletack saw them snooping around the house, he knew that he couldn't let them out of his sight. They were trouble, especially that sneaky Jared Grace!

All through that very first night, Thimbletack spied on the Graces.

When Jared found his way into Arthur's study, you can bet that Thimbletack was close on his heels!

The brownie watched with wide eyes as Jared found the Guide that he had hidden so carefully!

Thimbletack had to act fast! As quickly as he could, he scrawled a warning message in the dust on Arthur's desk, just where Jared would be sure to see it.

"JARED GRACE LEAVE THIS PLACE!" it read.

The mysterious message scared Jared.
He ran to his brother to show him the book.
Thimbletack followed Jared, but the boy
hid in a footlocker. It was too heavy to open!
The brownie decided to play a trick on
someone else.

"AHHHHHHHHHH!" screamed Mallory as Jared and Simon ran into their sister's room. There they found her, with her hair tied to the bedposts!

Thimbletack was a natural prankster,

and this was one of his best pranks yet. He knew that Jared would get blamed for this one! And maybe this would teach the meddlesome boy a lesson and he would stay away from the Guide.

Jared wanted to meet the naughty creature that had gotten him into trouble. So he set out a a treat that he knew Thimbletack wouldn't refuse—honey!

"Tasty, tasty, delicious honey," sang Thimbletack. "So good, so yummy, yummy, yummy."

After he had eaten his fill of honey, Thimbletack decided to talk to Jared. It was time to reveal the truth.

Thimbletack told Jared that it was his life's mission to keep the Guide safe. It was a promise he made to Arthur Spiderwick many years ago.

"Protect the book! And I did it, I hid it! I did my best, locked it in the chest!" he exclaimed. "But *you*, you looked and looked and found the book!"

"We must protect the book," Thimbletack told Jared. "Keep it in the circle!"

He pointed out the window to a ring of toadstools that surrounded Spiderwick Mansion.

Jared didn't know about the circle, so he looked it up in the Guide. It said that Arthur had put a charmed circle around the house to keep it safe.

"The Protective Circle protects the house, to protect the book?" asked Jared. "From who?"

"The ogre," Thimbletack said nervously, pointing out the window. "The lord of them!"

Jared had no idea what Thimbletack was talking about. He couldn't see anything outside!

Suddenly Thimbletack turned into a boggart and hurled a stone at him. There was a hole in the middle of the stone.

"Look through the stone," the boggart screamed. "Through the stone!"

Jared took his first look through the Seeing Stone. It was a magical tool that helped him see the invisible world. He was shocked to see lots of ugly froglike creatures. They were goblins! And they were right outside the circle—which meant they were right outside the house!

Now everything was out of control—the goblins were everywhere!

They captured Simon, who had been outside looking for his cat. But Jared was able to rescue his brother and bring him back to the mansion. At the house, Jared gave Mallory the Seeing Stone so she could see the creatures and help fight the goblins with her sword.

Thimbletack saw that Simon and Mallory were shocked to see him—a brownie living in their house!

But after Thimbletack told them about the evil ogre, Mulgarath, the Graces knew they had a bigger problem than a mischievous little brownie!

Thimbletack explained that Mulgarath wanted the secrets of the Guide so he could be all-powerful. He would rule the world!

Jared wasn't going let that happen. He had to come up with a plan. And suddenly he had an idea—Aunt Lucinda!

"She lived here, and it's her father's book," he said. "She can tell us what to do."

But there was a catch. They couldn't go outside the circle. The goblins were waiting for them!

Then the brownie told them, "Thimbletack knows a secret way, but in the house the book must stay."

Thimbletack trusted Jared to leave the Guide at the mansion, but the boy had other plans.

When the brownie wasn't looking, Jared slipped out of the house with the Guide under his jacket!

While Mallory and Jared went to talk to Aunt Lucinda, Simon and Thimbletack looked up ways to protect themselves against the goblins.

Simon found an old list. "Tomato sauce burns the skin, salt blinds them," he read. "Are there any more?" he asked Thimbletack. "What does the book say?"

And that's when the brownie discovered that Jared had tricked him!

"Eeeeek! Aaaaack!" screeched Thimbletack. Jared had replaced the Guide with a cookbook!

Simon was horrified to see Thimbletack transform into a boggart.

"Where's the boooook?" the boggart yelled.

Meanwhile a goblin attacked Jared and stole pages from the Guide. This meant that Mulgarath now knew how to break through the Protective Circle.

And sure enough, when Jared and Mallory came home, Mulgarath and the goblins

stormed Spiderwick mansion!

CRASH! BANG! BOOM! The battle raged all over the house.

Suddenly there was an explosion and tomato juice splattered all over the kitchen.

When all was quiet, Thimbletack peered out from his hiding place.

"Book safe?" he asked, just before Mulgarath appeared again! The ogre changed into a snake to crawl up to the study, but Thimbletack was ready. "Back off!" he growled, and he bit the snake. Mulgarath slithered away, then turned into a crow to catch the Guide, which Jared had tossed out the window.

Thimbletack watched in horror as the crow was about to grab the book with his claws, but then he smiled.

Hungry Hogsqueal, a hobgoblin, had been sitting in a tree by the window. He reached out to grab the bird—and ate it in two quick bites! Mulgarath and the goblins would never bother them again.

Thimbletack was beside himself with joy when Lucinda came to the mansion.

"Book safe, Lucy," he told her proudly.

"Yes, Thimbletack," Lucinda said. "If my father were here, he would say, 'Job well done.'"

And when Arthur Spiderwick magically returned, that is what he told Thimbletack. The brownie was pleased. His mission was complete!